DRAGON TALES

For Amelia

Judy Hayn

This is the second of the Dragon Tales Chronicles.
Already published:
Dragon Tales Book I: Quest for a Cave
Coming soon:
Dragon Tales Book III: Quest for Adventure
Dragon Tales Book IV: The Runaway

DRAGON TALES

BOOK II

Quest for a Friend

by

Judy Hayman

illustrated by

Caroline Wolfe Murray

First published in Great Britain by Practical
Inspiration Publishing, 2014

© Judy Hayman 2014
All illustrations by Caroline Wolfe Murray
The moral rights of the author and illustrator have
been asserted.

ISBN (print): 978-1-910056-15-8
ISBN (ebook): 978-1-910056-16-5

This one is for Elise, who gives me lots of good ideas.
J.L.H.

For my own dragonlets, Lily and Mabel.
C.W.M.

Table of Contents

Chapter 1

The Gloaming Huff

Emily the young dragon sat on the top of Ben McIlwhinnie's bald head at the end of a fine evening. Ben was a Scottish Mountain Giant, and the top of his head made an excellent lookout point. From here, Emily could look down the remote Highland glen to the loch, half hidden with trees and bushes, and the far-distant hills. It was wild and lonely with no sign of Humans anywhere, and Emily loved it.

It was the shock discovery that Humans were moving into their old glen that had forced the family to move. Emily shivered as she remembered the spooky night flight with her father when they had found a horrible wire fence, huge machines and even a nasty square building with a real live Human inside.

"Thank goodness we've got wings!" she thought, remembering their escape.

But now they had discovered Ben, and the cave under his huge rocky chair. She and her parents and younger brother Tom had found a safe new home.

The family had had a busy week; settling into the new cave, exploring the moorland leading up the mountains, foraging in the woods and swimming in the nearby loch with their new friends, the Otters. They were all delighted with their new home. Ben had gone back to sleep now, but he had made them promise to wake him up if anything important happened. "Good things or dangerous things, I don't mind which. A good strong huff should do it," he had said. Now Emily could hear the soft sighing of his breathing, sounding just like the wind. It reminded her that he was always there if she needed him.

She knew that Tom was quite content with his new life. He loved swimming with Lottie and Wattie, the young otter cubs, and spent as much time as he was allowed down at the loch diving and wallowing with a lot of noise. Emily wasn't such a good swimmer, but Mum had patiently coaxed her underwater, and although she was still not as confident as Tom, she was getting better at opening her eyes under the surface. She was fascinated by the teeming life in the loch, though the first time she had come nose to nose with a large trout she was startled into swallowing rather a lot of water. All the serious fishing had to be done at the other end of the loch these days, and the Ospreys, who had a nest at the top of a nearby tree, had given up in disgust and flown to a quieter one.

She loved having a cave to herself at night, and spent a lot of time reading, making plans and dreaming. She was quite friendly with the bats in her roof, though they were usually back in bed by the time she woke up in the morning, so they didn't really count as the kind of friends she needed.

Finding other dragons had become the most important thing to Emily. She thought of it as her New Quest, which sounded grand and as adventurous as her favourite stories. So she was very excited when she had learned about the Gloaming Huff.

After supper one night Dad had explained all about it.

"Mum and I never bothered back at our old cave," he had said, "but I know you'd like to see if there are other dragons around. Why not? This cave is higher than our old one, so it might be a good place for the Gloaming Huff."

"What's that?" Emily had asked, puzzled.

"Well, you know we often use smoke signalling," Dad had explained. "This is much the same, but you only do it in the evening. You go to the top of a hill and send a steady huff of smoke as high as you can, for as long as you can. Then you look all around to see if you can spot any other smoke. That's the Gloaming Huff. It's an ancient method of communication between dragons, and it's one that Humans don't notice, for some reason. There's quite a complicated code, so you can send messages once you've made contact. We could try if you like. You never know, some other dragon *might* spot our signal."

"Oh, please let's try!" Emily had exclaimed. So for the next three evenings, she and Dad had flown to the top of Ben's head and Dad had sent a straight huff high into the air. Then they had waited hopefully, gazing all around, until the light faded and it was Emily's bedtime. But there had been no answering smoke. Dad had decided it was a waste of time trying again, but Mum, who realised how disappointed Emily was, persuaded him to have one more Huff. This time, she and Dad huffed together, so their plume was higher and lasted longer, and Emily huffed too, just to feel she was helping.

Then Mum and Dad had gone back to the cave to make sure Tom cleaned his teeth before bed, but had allowed Emily to stay for a few more minutes, just in case.

"Any minute they'll call me down," she thought, "and it hasn't worked. I'll *never* find a friend!" She heaved a heavy sigh and then stood up as high as she could for a last look round. And then she saw it: a thin plume of white smoke far away to the south, just visible against the deepening blue of the evening sky.

"Dad, Dad!" she shouted. "Come quick! I've seen one!"

Both her parents flew up straight away and looked for the smoke. "Well spotted, Emily!" said Mum. "It's a long way away, but we must send an answer." She and Dad sent first a steady stream, and then a series of puffs.

"Right, that's all we can do for tonight," said Dad. "We've told them who we are and where to find us,

6

so we'll wait 'til tomorrow night and see if we get an answer."

Mum looked at Emily's beaming face. "Don't get too excited," she said gently. "We may hear nothing more. It might be a lonely old dragon, not the young friend you're hoping for. And it is a long way away. Bedtime now!"

All through the next day, while she foraged for snails and played in the woods with Tom and the little otters, Emily saw again in her mind that thin plume of smoke and wondered who had huffed it. She was too excited to eat much supper, and as soon as the sun set the whole family flew up to Ben's head. Tom perched on his favourite ear as usual. They all gazed south, and in a few minutes the smoke was seen again, but nearer – much nearer.

"He says he's on his way," said Dad, after he had studied the signals, "but that's all. Nothing about who he is, or whether he's on his own. I'll send a reply." He

7

huffed busily, and Mum explained that he was telling the strange dragon he'd be welcome and sending directions. Two tiny puffs were sent in return.

"I bet that says O.K." said Tom.

Dad laughed. "More or less," he said, "but he won't be here for a while, so an early night for us all, I think, and we'll see what sort of dragon turns up tomorrow!"

"I'll never get to sleep!" Emily declared, but her parents only laughed and shooed her firmly into her bedroom.

Chapter 2

Desmond

The next morning Emily was up long before anybody else, but there was no sign of a visitor. She was disappointed, but set about preparing porridge for breakfast as a nice surprise for the others.

Dad was up next. "Don't worry, he'll come," he said, seeing Emily stirring slowly with her wings drooping sadly. "Let's give your mother breakfast in bed. She's feeling a bit tired this morning."

It was after breakfast, while Tom was arguing that it wasn't his turn to wash up, that it happened. Emily gasped and pointed. Flying slowly towards them was the strangest shaped creature she had ever seen. It certainly didn't look like a dragon! As soon as he saw it, Dad flew up to investigate, and they watched breathlessly as he met the creature, flew over and around it, and then waved cheerfully to them. A few minutes later he landed beside them, and so did the stranger, with a loud clanking noise, which brought Mum out of bed in a hurry.

It *was* a dragon! Hung around him, dangling from spikes and claws, was a strange assortment of bags and bundles which explained his odd shape in the sky. When he had unhooked them all they could see him clearly. He looked weary but grinned round at them all cheerfully.

"Hi! Got your message. I'm Desmond. Des. Glad to meet you. It's been quite a flight."

"Breakfast?" asked Mum, sounding a bit dazed.

"That'd be great, thanks," said the strange dragon. He flopped on the ground, put his head down between his front legs, shut his eyes and heaved a mighty huff. A wavering smoke ring drifted away down the hill. Dad signalled to Tom to fetch him some water from the stream, and Emily followed Mum into the cave.

"Leave him alone for a few minutes to get his breath back, and help me to get him some breakfast," said Mum. "There'll be plenty of time for questions later."

After several long drinks and some food, Desmond recovered a little. Emily had been sneaking looks at him while she helped Mum, and thought he was the weirdest dragon she had ever seen. He had a small gold hoop in one ear! She thought he was dark green, but he was so grubby it was hard to be sure. But the tips of all his spikes were different colours – vivid orange, yellow, purple, blue – and the spiky end of his tail was bright red. His wings had black, white and red stripes. She had never heard of rainbow dragons! He was quite young, but fully grown – nearly as big as Dad.

"I'm travelling," he explained when he had finished a large breakfast and they had introduced themselves properly. "I'm much too young to settle down! I've flown all over the place. Last year I spent quite a while in the mountains way over in the East. There are some amazing dragons in the forests there, and they're *mostly* friendly. Spent the winter further south, where the sea is warm and there are lots of sandy beaches. The problem is there are far too many Humans and not many dragons, so you have to be careful where you land. I had to do most of my flying over England at night and watch out for those noisy Human flying machines. Fortunately you can always hear them coming and dodge. I think I was sighted a couple of times, but nothing serious. I had a feeling Scotland might be a bit quieter, so I was heading north when I spotted your signal. I've met a few dragon families on the way, but not many."

"Are you from Wales originally?" asked Mum. "You look green – at least mostly green! My mother is Welsh, and I used to live there. My parents still do. I haven't seen them for a long time. Their cave is near Cader Idris in the north."

"You don't mean Nan and Edward?" Mum nodded eagerly. "Wow! That's a coincidence! They are great old dragons. Nan is the sparkiest dragon I know. She told me lots about the world before I went off travelling. She knows *everything*."

"She reads a lot," Mum said proudly, with shining eyes. "She taught me and I taught Emily."

"Really?" said Desmond, looking at Emily admiringly and making her blush. "Cool!"

"If you're a friend of Nan, you had better stay for a bit," Mum decided. "We've enough room. You probably need to sleep, but how about a good wash first? Emily and Tom will take you down to the loch."

The children jumped up eagerly, though they were still feeling a bit shy, and the three of them spread their wings and flew down to the loch.

"Hey, wow! Great lake!" Desmond cried. He flew up high, folded his wings and dived, snout first, into the deepest water. There was a fountain of splash and four otter heads appeared on the surface, bobbing and spluttering.

"Wha' on earth wuz tha'? Ye'll be havin' the fish dying o' shock! Surely no' yer Da? He kens how ter fish!"

"Sorry," said Emily, landing on a rock that jutted into the loch. "It was our new friend, Des. He's just arrived. I hope he's all right. He's been down there a long time."

Tom dived in, looked around and came up again, blowing bubbles. "Can't see him," he said.

Emily was starting to look worried when there was a great flurry a little way down the loch, and Desmond surfaced, whirled around with his wings outstretched, and dived again. The otters sighed. "Ah hope he'll no' be stayin' long!" they said, and swam away, leaving Wattie and Lottie behind.

"He's a Traveller," Tom boasted. "He's flown all over the world. He's dead cool!" He and the young otters joined Emily on her rock and settled down to watch out for Desmond. Soon he surfaced and swam over to join them. He looked a good deal cleaner, Emily thought, and he *was* green, dark with a paler tummy.

He still had his rainbow spikes, but one or two of them had run a little. Lottie and Wattie stared in surprise.

"Why're ye aa diff'rent colours?" asked Wattie. "Is it camouflage like?"

"I dyed them. I used to paint them black, but I had these colours done in the South. I'll show you how if you like," he added to Emily and Tom, stretching his stripy wings to dry in the sun.

"Yuck, no thanks," said Tom, but Emily secretly liked the idea, even though she was fond of her particular shade of purply-blue with the paler pinkish wings.

Desmond turned to the little otters. "Fancy a fly around?" he asked.

"Yeah!" they shouted together. Emily had a nasty feeling that none of the parents would approve, but before she could say anything, Lottie and Wattie had scrambled onto Desmond's back and were clinging fast to his spikes. They took off, with Tom flying close behind, and Emily decided she had better follow in case they went too high.

"No worries!" Desmond shouted to her. "I'll stay over the water so even if they fall off they'll be OK!"

16

He flew away down the loch and wheeled round sharply while the cubs shrieked in delight. Then he flew low, neatly tipped the pair of them into the water and soared away, laughing. Emily and Tom started to follow, then saw all four parents standing in a line on the bank watching in disapproval.

"Ah *really* hope he isnae stayin' long!" said the twins' dad. His cubs scrambled out of the water, shook themselves and disagreed.

"He's cool, Da'!" yelled Wattie. "Can we fly again? Can we?"

"Can I learn to dive like that?" Tom demanded. "Can I?"

Dad sighed and looked at his wife. "Are you *sure* it was a good idea to ask him to stay?"

Emily looked anxiously at both of them, but Mum smiled. "I think he'll fit in just fine, don't you, Emily?" she said, handing round bumblebugs.

"Wow, bumbugs! Haven't had them for ages!" said Des, coming back and taking two.

Tom shrieked in delight. "BUMBUGS!" he yelled to the otters, and belly-flopped into the loch.

Des sat down beside Mum and Emily, crunching noisily. "This is a great spot. Yeah, think I might stay for a bit, if that's OK with you?" he said.

"As long as you don't ruin the fishing completely," said Dad, flying off to reassure the otters.

"I think we could cope with having you to stay!" Mum said, and Emily beamed at them happily. "Good for the Gloaming Huff!" she thought to herself. "It worked!"

Chapter 3

Desmond's Big Idea

It was great fun having Desmond staying with them. He slept outside the cave, wrapped in a grubby bag and sheltered from the wind by the gorse bush. He helped with the cooking, and produced some *very* peculiar meals using special hot seeds and pods he had picked up on his travels. He took turns with the washing up. Best of all, he spent a lot of time with Emily and Tom, and took them exploring in the hills as well as swimming and diving in the loch with the otters. They even ventured down the glen to the ruins of the ancient castle that Ben had told them about on their first night. Mum and Dad were pleased, because Mum was still feeling rather tired, and not up to long flights, so they stayed behind when the three went off for the day. There was still a lot to do in the new cave, they said.

Desmond was a fund of wonderful stories; so good that Emily almost forgot about her books. He had once had a fight with eagles in the mountains and damaged his wings. He had encountered a fierce bear when lost in a forest – though it actually turned out to be friend-ly and took him home to meet the family. He'd spied on Humans many times, and even been kidnapped by pirates! (Mum and Dad were a bit doubtful about this last one, but Emily believed it and Tom was thrilled.)

Emily particularly liked it when he talked about the sea, and wished she could see that huge loch that went on forever, where the water rose up in high waves and exploded on the shore. It made their loch seem rather tame. Lottie and Wattie, who listened to some of the stories too, started pestering their parents to take them to the sea.

"Can we wake Ben to let him meet Des?" Emily asked on the second day. "He did say we could if something important happened."

"Certainly not, he's only just gone back to sleep," said Mum.

Desmond looked disappointed. He had been taken up to perch on Ben's head, and was looking forward to seeing the giant awake and moving. "You're so lucky!" he said. "I've travelled all over, but I've *never* met a real ancient Mountain Giant. Are you sure we couldn't try one little huff up his nose?"

"Don't you dare!" said Mum. "One huff and you're banished. We'll only wake Ben when there's something *really* important to show him."

"Will you stay with us forever?" Emily asked one day, as she and Desmond sat on Ben's head after supper.

Tom was practising acrobatics on Ben's ears and she had been talking to Des about her grandparents, Nan and Edward. She had met them once, before Tom was hatched. Nan was Welsh green and Edward was dark Scottish blue, but with touches of gold on his wings and spikes that suggested traces of Irish ancestry. They both told wonderful stories, and Nan could sing too. She loved them and wished they lived a bit nearer.

"Can't do that, I'm a Traveller," said Desmond. "It's been great, but I'll have to be off soon." Emily looked so forlorn that he felt sorry for her. "But I've had an idea. I met a really nice family on my way here. They were living in a patch of forest – there weren't any decent caves around – and they had to keep moving on in case Humans found them. I'm sure they'd like it better up here. Why don't I try to Huff them for you? I know you'd like some dragon neighbours!"

Emily was excited at once. "How many were there? Were they nice?" She wanted to ask if there was a girl of her age, but she didn't dare, in case she was disappointed.

Desmond grinned. He knew what she was thinking. "There *was* a girl about the same age as you, with two brothers, two parents and a grandpa. I liked them."

"What colour were they?" Emily asked breathlessly.

"Red – well, orange really, and sort of pinkish round the edges. Not like the dark red wild dragons I've seen abroad. You wouldn't want one of *those* living near you! Let's see what your Mum and Dad think. I'll talk to them tonight when you've gone to bed."

Emily had to be content to wait, but she went to bed feeling excited. Des was a very nice friend to have, but a pinkish-orange girl dragon would be even better!

The next morning Dad said that he and Mum liked the idea and they had been making plans. "Des says that there's a good Huffing hill a day's flight south of here. From there we should be able to contact this family he's told us about. How would you two like to go on a long flight tomorrow with Des and me? We can camp overnight and come back the next day." He glanced at Mum, who nodded.

"Don't you want to come?" Emily asked Mum.

"Not this time. You'll be fine with Dad and Des to give you the occasional lift, and you can tell me all about it when you get back."

"Brilliant!" Tom shouted and rushed off down the hill to boast to the otter twins. Des went to check his camping gear, but Emily followed Mum into the cave. "Are you sure you're all right? You've been very tired lately," she said.

Mum smiled and gave her a loving huff. "I'm just fine! I'll enjoy two peaceful days by myself. Go and have fun with the others."

The next morning Des hooked on some travelling gear and they set off. They flew low over the loch, and the little otters waved as they passed. "They wanted to come too," said Tom as they headed south. "Pity they can't fly!"

Desmond led them on a winding flight path that avoided any places where they might be seen by Humans. They flew high, but once they were spotted by a group of brightly-dressed Humans walking up a lonely glen. They could hear faint exclamations of surprise as they flew over as fast as they could.

"No worries!" said Desmond, "No-one will believe them if they go back and say they've seen dragons. Humans know dragons don't exist. It's very useful! We'll be far away by the time anyone comes looking."

They got to Desmond's hill as the sun was setting, and hurried to light a fire. While supper was cooking, they gathered on the summit and Desmond sent up a signal. In a few minutes there was a faraway answering puff, and Dad and Desmond started to send more complicated messages, and read the distant huffs and puffs that they could see in the sky. Tom and Emily stared in amazement, but knew better than to interrupt. "I must get Dad to teach me Huff," Emily thought, as there was a final burst of small white dots.

Dad turned to them. "Right, all settled. We'll tell you about it over supper. You go down with the children, Des. I want to send a quick huff to Gwen." Desmond nodded, and led them to the sheltered hollow where the supper was almost ready. In a few minutes Dad joined them. "She's fine," he said. Desmond looked relieved, which puzzled Emily. She wondered if they had a secret that they weren't telling her and Tom, but forgot about it in her hurry to hear about the Huffs.

They ate a spicy slug stew and finished up with mint tea (Des had found a patch of wild mint, and Emily decided she liked it better than their usual nettle brew). Then Dad told them that the new family seemed keen to meet them and had suggested that they all gather at a place called 'Safari Park' to discuss things.

"I know where that is," said Desmond. "It's a weird place, quite a way south of here. There are lions and elephants and all sorts of strange creatures kept in cages by Humans. No dragons, though. There are always hordes of Humans around during the day but it's safe at night. There are no Humans around then, and the other animals are OK, if you're careful. I'll take you there. When?"

"Soon as we can. It will fit perfectly!" He grinned at Desmond happily.

"What about Mum?" asked Emily, and was relieved when Dad said that she would be coming too. She had begun to worry a little.

"We'll stay here tomorrow," Dad said. "I'm a bit bothered about those Humans that saw us on the way here. No point risking being spotted again. We'll go home overnight. You can give Tom a lift, can't you, Des? I can take Emily."

"I can fly myself!" said Tom, but Dad explained that fast night flying was very tricky, and he would need a lift for part of the way, at least. They were tired after their long day, so very soon they all curled up beside the smouldering fire, and settled down to sleep. Emily tried to count the stars, but soon fell asleep and dreamed of friendly new dragons and stamping elephants until morning.

Chapter 4

The Waterfall

The night flight home seemed very short, because both Tom and Emily were tired after a busy day climbing and foraging with Dad and Des. They had gathered lots of wild mint, some particularly juicy slugs and found a lot of birds' nests on the ground. (They were careful to take only one egg from each nest, knowing that birds can't usually count.) Des packed it all carefully so they could carry it home.

They set out as dusk was falling, and very soon Tom drooped and climbed onto Des's back. Emily flew a little longer, then she too accepted a lift with Dad, settled herself comfortably between his wings and fell asleep. She woke once, when the full moon rose and shone into her eyes, but the steady beat of her father's wings lulled her back to sleep. Tom didn't even wake up when they arrived home as dawn was breaking, and had to be carried into his room, snoring gently, his head and tail dangling.

Emily did wake up, smiled sleepily at Mum, and crawled into her heather bed. Just before she fell asleep again, she heard quiet voices outside her room. "Is it OK?" That was Dad, and Mum whispered, "It's well wrapped up, quite safe, in the Bone Cave. Go and take a peep." Emily was too sleepy to wonder what they were talking about, and when she woke later in the morning she thought she had dreamed it.

The next two days were very busy, as they prepared for their trip to Safari Park. For some reason it seemed important *exactly* when they started and came back. Mum made the decision after she had consulted Des. "Six days away," she said. "Four days travelling, there and back, two days there. That should be enough. So we have to start the day after tomorrow. We can be ready if you all help to pack."

Dad collected a lot of new bracken and heather and carried it carefully into the Bone Cave, saying that they needed a good stock while it was nice and dry. He said he didn't need any help with that, to Emily's surprise. All their belongings were stored at the back of the cave, and Des scythed some big branches of gorse with his tail to cover the entrance in case of explorers. Emily was pleased to see that he had piled a few of his bundles with their things. It meant that he would have to come back for them. She was a bit afraid that he would be tempted to start travelling again.

The evening before they set off, Desmond, Tom and Emily went down to the loch for a last swim with the otters. Emily had a feeling that the otter parents were looking forward to a peaceful week's fishing, but Wattie and Lottie were very sad that they were going away. They begged Des to take them flying one more time.

"Ri' doon the valley?" Wattie begged. "No' jist o'er the loch. Tha's boring!"

Desmond shook his head. "Too dangerous over land," he said. "If you fell you'd go splat! Over the water you'll only go splosh."

"Loop the loop then?" pleaded Lottie. So the little otters clung to Desmond's coloured spikes with all eight feet, and he took them up and down the loch, soaring and looping until they squealed with laughter and finally dropped off into the water. Desmond dived after them.

Tom and Emily practised looping too, and Emily tried her first nose-dive, though not a very high one. She was pleased with herself, though it took a while to rid her nose of water. Tom, who had been watching how the otters fished, tried a long underwater swim and managed to catch a small fish in his mouth.

Tired but happy, and a good deal cleaner than usual, they said goodnight to the otters and flew back to the cave for hot mint tea and early bed.

The next day they all flew south, high over rocky hills, heathery moors and tumbling rivers, keeping close together. As Dad said, if they *were* spotted, they would just look like a rather peculiar shape in the sky, not like five dragons at all. Towards evening they glided down to a lonely valley beside a wide river, far bigger than any river the young dragons had seen before. They could hear roaring water nearby.

"I think that's a waterfall," said Desmond. "A big one, by the sound of it. I'll cook supper, if you like, while you four go and find it."

They helped him to build a fire and then set off towards the sound. As they scrambled round some

32

high rocks they saw a high white wall of water, falling sheer into a deep green pool. Spray soaked them all, and felt cool and fresh after their long flight. Emily and Tom jumped and danced with delight.

"Can we swim in the pool?" yelled Tom over the roar of the water.

"Yes!" shouted Dad, and all four leapt in. Emily was glad she had practised her swimming, as the pool shelved steeply and there was no shallow water at the edge. Mum swam right under the waterfall, and let the water cascade over her head. The water was so clear that Emily could see the shape of Dad swimming in circles under water. Tom rolled and dived. Emily swam to the edge and let the water spray over her, but she was careful not to get under the main fall.

When they heard a shout above them, they all surfaced and looked up. "DRAGONIMO!!" yelled Desmond, and flew straight through the middle of the waterfall. They all gasped, expecting to see him caught and dashed down into the pool, but he shot through and out the other side, wheeled round and

33

plunged through again. Then he landed on a high rock and shook his wings.

"Fantastic!" he shouted. "Best waterfall I've flown through in ages. Try it!" Dad caught Tom by the tail as he was preparing to launch himself to join Desmond.

"No you don't!" he said. "You'd be swept down for sure. Keep hold of him," he added to Mum, passing Tom's tail over. Then he flew up and soared through the fall too. Desmond cheered.

Tom and Emily were impressed, but Mum sighed. "He's just trying to prove he's not too old!" she said. "Right you two, back to the fire to get dry." Their wings were too thoroughly soaked to fly, so they scrambled down the path to their camp, and soon Dad and Desmond joined them. "I'm starving!" said Tom and Des together.

Desmond had cooked snake sausages on sticks over the fire, and a dip to go with them that was so hot and spicy that they all sat around afterwards huffing flames. Tom was delighted because for the first time he produced a tiny spark. "I'm glad I had a second helping," he said. "It looks as if I'm getting old enough!" He and Desmond wandered off into the trees for Tom to practise huffs before bed.

Tom was keen to camp by the waterfall for a few days, but to Emily's relief, Mum and Dad said they must stick to their plan and travel on. Dad promised to camp there on the way home, so obviously he liked the waterfall too.

They had to be more careful on the next day's flight, as they saw more signs of humans below them, but fortunately it was quite a cloudy day. At first Emily liked the spooky feeling of flying through cloud, but soon she got bored, and preferred the clear patches of sky. They saw more towns and villages than the children had ever seen before, and the roads with tiny speeding vehicles were exciting, even though they knew they were dangerous. They flew higher than birds, though they saw a few wheeling buzzards, who were very curious and called all their friends to see them with strange mewing cries

By the end of the afternoon they were all tired. Desmond said he would take them to a patch of forest that he remembered near Safari Park where they could rest while he made contact with the other dragons. They zigzagged down to earth and landed safely in the middle of the trees. Mum insisted that Tom and Emily had a nap, in case they were in for a busy night. They were so tired that they didn't protest at all!

Chapter 5

Midnight Meeting

W hen Mum woke them up it was dark. Desmond had come back, and he and Dad were making plans.

"As soon as the moon is up, we'll go," said Desmond as they crunched a hasty supper of snails. "We're to meet them by the lake. It isn't far. They're really excited."

Emily was too. She felt quivery and didn't feel like eating.

"We must be very careful of the animals," Desmond continued. "Some of them sleep at night, but lots don't. There are big square beasts with dragonish horns on their noses that I wouldn't want to mess with. Watch out for the roaring ones – lions they're called. They roam about and if there are little ones the females can be very fierce. The huge ones with long noses are . . ."

"Elephants," Emily interrupted eagerly, "I've read about them."

"Yes, well they shouldn't cause us much trouble, but mind you don't get trodden on!"

"The biggest problem will be Humans," Dad warned. "At the first sign of one, get out fast!"

"Yes, they'd like nothing better than to capture us and put us in cages," Desmond agreed.

Mum was looking doubtful. "Are you sure we should take the children, Duncan? Couldn't Des bring the other dragons here?"

"NO!" said Tom and Emily together, and Tom added, "I want to see Nellyfants!"

"We'll all go," Dad decided. "But tonight we'll keep together, and just meet up with the other dragons. We might have a chance of more exploring tomorrow night. Do you hear me, Tom? No going off on your own looking for Nellyfants!" Tom scowled, but agreed, reluctantly.

The moon was up by the time they landed on a smooth patch of grass by a small lake. A family of ducks made a great fuss and flapped off noisily. They looked round nervously, ready to fly up at once if any lions, elephants or Humans came along, but all they heard were chattering cries coming from some trees across the lake. "Only monkeys," whispered Desmond. "But where are the dragons?"

They all looked around. Emily felt her heart beating fast. Then, from a patch of bushes a little further along the shore, they saw two shapes, keeping low to the ground, creeping towards them. Emily pressed close to Mum, who held out a claw. The shapes came nearer, until eventually Emily could make out the outlines of two grown-up dragons. She was so disappointed that she felt like bursting into tears, but Desmond went forward to meet them.

"Hi there," he said cheerfully, "nice to see you again. I've brought this lot, as I promised. Gwen and Duncan, meet Oliver and Ellen."

Mum and Dad shook claws with the two new dragons. "Our youngest is Tom and this is Emily," said Dad. "I thought you had children too?"

"We have," said Ellen, "but we decided it would be safer to leave them with Oliver's dad." Emily breathed a sigh of relief and Ellen smiled at her. "My Alice is looking forward to meeting you," she said.

"Why don't you all come back with us," said Oliver. "We've a safe camping place in the forest where we can meet and talk properly. It's not far, and there's room for you all."

"That OK with you?" Desmond asked them.

Emily nodded eagerly and Mum and Dad agreed, but Tom protested. "I want to see the Nellyfants!"

Oliver grinned at him. "Tomorrow night. We'll all come for a proper explore, I promise. Come on. It's not far."

They all spread their wings and he led the way over the park towards the forest. Five lions looked up and roared at them as they passed, but there was no sign of Tom's 'nellyfants'. Soon they were gliding down to a clearing in the middle of a forest, where a cheerful fire was glowing. Another dragon looked up and waved a wing as they all followed Oliver to land.

"Welcome," he said. "I'm George." He was an elderly dragon, with wrinkled skin that was quite grey, though his wings were still a reddish colour and his face looked wise and kindly. Emily liked the look of him.

"The children are asleep," he said. "At least I thought they were!" he added, as two smaller shapes crept up to the fire. "Alice and Ollie, who said you could get up?"

"Oh, Grandad!" said the girl, whose skin glowed bright orange in the firelight. "It's far too exciting to sleep!"

"Hot drinks for everyone, and I've got some wasp waffles with honey," said Ellen. "Sit down and make yourselves at home. Is Georgie still asleep? He's not two yet," she added to Mum.

Emily sat down, feeling suddenly shy. She had wanted to meet a new girl dragon for so long, but now she didn't know what to say. Tom was quiet too, which was not like him at all. The boy dragon looked quite a bit bigger than him, deep orange-red like his father, and he had greeted Desmond like an old friend, clapping wings in a High Four and huffing sparks with delight.

Oliver was talking to Dad. "We've been on the move for months. Ellen and I have never really had a settled home, and we like travelling, but it's more difficult now George is getting older and we have another little one. But it's hard to find a safe place to settle down. There are no mountains in the South, so caves are hard to find, unless you're by the sea, and that's always swarming with Humans. We usually live in forests, like this, but even that's getting more dangerous. Have you always lived up north? I thought the place was covered with snow all the time."

Dad laughed and explained that, although it snowed in winter, it wasn't too bad the rest of the time. He told them about the mountains and the lochs, the woods and the moors and then he described their cave, though he didn't mention Ben McIlwhinnie. The dragons sat close round the fire to listen. Then Emily realised that Alice had crept round to sit beside her.

"I've never seen a proper cave, but I've read about them," she whispered. "Do you like living in a cave? I think I'd miss sleeping in the open air. I like counting stars before I go to sleep."

Emily gasped. "Do you read books too?"

"Oh yes," said Alice, "but I haven't had a new one for ages. I'll show you tomorrow. You are staying, aren't you?"

"Just for a day or two, then we have to go home," said Emily.

"I think you children should go to bed," said Ellen firmly.

Mum agreed. "You've come a long way today, and if you want to explore tomorrow night, you need your sleep. Alice and Ollie will find you a cosy spot. See you in the morning." She huffed a goodnight kiss and they went to settle down in the long grass with the others.

Emily peeped at a small curled-up dragonlet. "Is that your wee brother? He looks really cute!" Alice whispered back, "He is, but sometimes he's a pest! Brothers are, aren't they? Goodnight."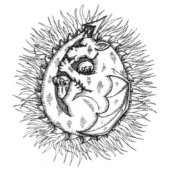

Chapter 6

A Day of Exploring

The grown-ups must have stayed round the fire for quite a long time that night, drinking Firewater and talking, because in the morning, after a very late breakfast, they gathered the children around and explained their plans.

"We've decided we'll head north with Gwen and Duncan," Oliver said. "The weather up there doesn't sound as bad as we've always been told."

"Fewer Humans around will be a real advantage," said old George.

"We'll camp out in the woods near their cave," added Ellen. "Then if we all like living near each other, we might look for a cave for the winter. What do you children think?"

Emily was so delighted that she couldn't think of anything to say. She just beamed at Alice, who smiled back happily.

"Sounds OK," said Ollie. "Is Des coming too?"

Emily held her breath, hoping that Des would say yes.

"For a bit," he said. "It's a great place you've got, but there's a lot more of the world to see. I'll come up and see you settled, though."

"We're not going to start at once are we?" said Tom anxiously. "What about the Nellyfants?"

Ollie laughed at him, but old George smiled. "You can have a proper explore of the Park tonight, as soon as the humans leave. We'll find your 'nellyfants' for you."

"Today you children can play around in the forest, but don't stray too far and stay away from paths. Keep a look-out for any rambling Humans and if you see any, hide AT ONCE. No jokey huffs at them, Ollie. I mean it! There are too many of us here to hide safely."

While they talked, the little dragonlet, Geor-gie, bounced around with squeaks and huffs. Emily hoped she would have a chance to play with him, but Alice whispered, "Come on, we'll show you the best bits of the forest," and the four children dashed away, leaving Georgie and the grown-ups behind.

It was a lovely day. Emily and Alice sat by a stream, dangling their tails in the cool water, and talked. Alice had lots of interesting stories to tell about her travels, and Emily felt that her life so far had been very dull by comparison. The best stories were about the sea, and Emily remembered all that Desmond had told her and wished and wished that she could go and see it.

They joined the two boys in a project to dam the stream, though as Alice pointed out, there wasn't much point in creating a swimming pool when they were leaving the next day. Tom told them all about the loch and swimming with the otters, and was pleased to discover that Ollie and Alice hadn't done as much swimming as he had. Ollie seemed so much older and more daring, and he didn't want to be left behind in *everything*.

They saw no Humans, which disappointed Ollie, but at lunchtime Desmond joined them, carrying Georgie and snacks for them all.

"We're having a very early supper so that we can have a longer time to explore the Park," he said. "But we don't need to go back just yet." He joined the boys in a riotous game of Knights 'n' Dragons while Emily and Alice splashed in the stream with Georgie.

"I sometimes get fed up looking after my little brother, but it's much more fun when you have a friend to share him with," said Alice, and Emily felt a glow of happiness spread through her. At last she had a friend to share things with! Alice was coming back with her to Ben's mountain – and surely when they arrived, Mum and Dad would agree that Ben could be woken up. She would share Ben with Alice!

That evening they all set off quietly for Safari Park, leaving George behind to look after his little grandson. Desmond went ahead to check that it was safe, then they made their way cautiously, flying low and creeping. They had to cross a 'Road', which even Mum and Dad had never done before, and the sight of Human machines roaring past so close to their hiding place was extremely scary! When they were all safely across, they made their way in a line along a high hedge to the first open space of the Park.

Here there were herds of deer, which were not nearly as impressive as the ones at home, Emily thought. She discovered that Alice had never seen big Scottish deer. But there were huge shaggy beasts as well, and strange humpy creatures, which she thought were called Camerels. Then she had a shock. In a small shelter were three huge eggs.

"Mum!" she called. "There are dragon eggs here! Look!"

Everyone came to see. "Not dragon eggs," said Ellen, "but far too big for ordinary birds. I wonder whose they are."

A thumping noise made them all turn round, and they spotted two strange creatures running very fast towards them. They had long legs and necks and

round fluffy bodies, and they did *not* look friendly! "UP!" shouted Dad and Oliver together, and they all took flight, just in time to avoid fierce pecks. Desmond and Ollie delayed, trying to frighten them by dancing up and down in the air and huffing. At the last minute, they tried to fly up, but too late! Desmond got two sharp pecks on his tail as he took off and dripped blood as he flew away, but Ollie's tail was caught fast in the strong beak of the leading ostrich, and however hard he flapped his wings, he couldn't get free.

"HELP!" he yelled, so Desmond turned back and huffed smoke into the eyes of the bird, until it was forced to let go. Ollie's tail was kinked above the spike, and very sore.

"It serves you right!" said his Dad. "Stop showing off. And Des, don't encourage him!" Desmond grinned sheepishly.

They flew over the big enclosure where the lions were prowling, without stopping but low enough to get a good view of shaggy manes and wide mouths with sharp teeth. "Keep Out!" said Oliver sternly to his son. "Yes, KEEP OUT, whatever you are!!" roared the largest lion, shaking his mane at them.

They landed beyond the lions' enclosure and gathered round while Oliver pointed out the possible dangers. "We can split up and explore this part as long as you children ALWAYS keep a grown-up in sight. Then we'll go together to the elephants, Tom. Any problems, especially Humans, don't wait around - fly!"

Emily spotted a notice saying 'Otters' and rushed over, but the pen looked empty. "They must be asleep somewhere," she thought. She looked at the small stream and tiny pool in the enclosure and thought of the speed of the free otters in their own wild loch. It made her feel sad, so she hurried past.

"I'd hate to be trapped like that," she said to Alice, who agreed.

"If we lived here, we'd be put in a cage with a roof of wire to stop us flying away," she said. "There are owls over there, but I hate looking at them because they can't fly properly. It must be awful!"

Emily shuddered. "I think I'll be glad to get back to my mountains," she said. "This place is a bit too Humanish for me!"

Next they found a cage full of small monkeys, who gathered at the wire in surprise. Emily read "Marmosets" on a notice, and thought they looked really cute, with their big eyes and comical white whiskers. "Don't you hate living in a cage?" asked Alice, but the marmosets told them that they were let out to roam around during the day, but preferred their warm cosy cage at night.

"But what about the Humans?" said Emily in horror.

The marmosets chuckled. "They're no trouble! Far too slow and clumsy. We can run faster and climb and swing in the trees. See them catch us! And they've been warned that we bite, so *they're* quite scared of *us!*" A few young ones made faces and bared their pointed teeth then giggled, and the dragons laughed too.

Desmond came across. "We're going to look for the elephants," he said. "Coming?"

They joined the others. Tom was in a state of wild excitement. "We huffed at stripy lions!" he said to Emily, then rushed ahead with Ollie.

"I think Ollie might be a bad influence on Tom," Alice said quietly to Emily in a grown-up voice, and Emily agreed.

To their disappointment, there was no sign of any elephants in the big enclosure where they lived, just trees and bushes, a small pond and a huge stack of hay. Desmond offered to show the girls the tigers, while the grown-ups went to chat to the owls. Mum wondered if there was any way of freeing them from their cages.

Suddenly they all heard a loud yell from the direction of the elephant field. They rushed across and saw a dreadful sight. The big haystack was blazing fiercely, and there was no sign of Tom and Ollie at all!

Chapter 7

Fire!

"Tom! Ollie!" Mum shouted, and she and Ellen flew into the enclosure to search frantically, while Des and the Dads tried to jump the fire out. But it was no good, it had taken hold and now smoke and flames were rising high into the air.

"We have to leave!" yelled Oliver.

Suddenly they heard a pounding of heavy feet and Emily and Alice, watching in horror from behind the fence, saw two huge elephants, trunks raised and ears flapping, stomping fast across the field.

"MOVE AWAY!" one called in a deep voice, and the dragons retreated. Both elephants filled their trunks from the pond and sent powerful streams of water onto the fire. Again and again they squirted, until the flames were out and all that was left was a blackened, smoking heap. The dragons watched, too scared to move.

The elephants lowered their trunks and turned themselves slowly around to face the group of frightened dragons.

"WHO STARTED THAT?" asked the bigger of the two.

"THAT WAS OUR HAY!" said the second, waving a menacing trunk.

"I don't know," said Dad bravely, stepping forward. "I admit we *can* huff flames when we want to, but none of us was near the haystack."

"Unless . . ." said Oliver. "Where are the boys?"

"Here!" said a voice, and from behind the smouldering haystack came Gwen and Ellen, each dragging a filthy boy by the tail. They dropped them in front of the elephants, but stood behind them with their wings raised, ready to protect their offspring if necessary. Alice gasped and Emily held her breath.

"WAS THAT YOU?" said the elephant to the quivering young dragons.

"Y-yes," admitted Ollie. "You see, Tom is only just learning to Huff, so I was showing him how I did it, and we were practising on a bit of the hay and then he tried really hard and he managed his very first proper Huff, but it was stronger than we expected, and the hay caught fire and I tried to put it out but that only made things worse, and ... "

"What have I told you about fires?" demanded Oliver furiously.

"I know, but ..."

"No buts! It was a stupid thing to do! You should know better at your age."

"Tom!" said Mum sternly, "what do you say?"

"S..sorry!" said Tom in a trembling voice, not daring to look up at the elephants. Emily was starting to feel sorry for him. He looked very small and defenceless beside the elephants.

"H-MM," said the first elephant sternly. "I THINK YOU BOTH NEED A LESSON!" He winked at the parents, just to show that there was no real danger, but the two boys had put their wings over their eyes, so didn't see. They thought of huge feet trampling and long trunks whipping and trembled. Emily and Alice were worried too, and screwed their eyes shut.

Then they heard a loud burst of water. Both elephants had filled their trunks again and squirted a fierce jet of water over both boys, soaking them thoroughly. They looked pathetic, drenched and shivering, pinned to the ground.

"THAT SHOULD PUT OUT YOUR FLAMES FOR A WHILE!" said one elephant, and they both watched as the dripping boys crawled slowly to join the others. Alice and Emily tried not to giggle, but Desmond roared with laughter, and that made the boys feel even worse.

"Thank you!" said Mum to the elephants.

"And we're really sorry about your hay," added Ellen.

"WE'LL BE GIVEN MORE. NO REAL HARM DONE," said one. "WE DON'T GET MUCH EXCITEMENT IN HERE, SO COME AGAIN!"

Suddenly they all heard a loud NEE - NAW! NEE - NAW! Flashing blue lights were coming nearer and nearer. At the same moment there were shouts and the dazzling beams of torches and several Humans could be seen in the distance, running towards them.

The elephants raised their heads. "QUICK, FLY AWAY! THEY'VE SEEN THE SMOKE. GO!!" The dragons flew and scattered, too frightened to know where they were heading. The boys were too wet to fly properly and struggled to take off.

"Des, Duncan, give the boys a lift," Oliver shouted. "Follow me. Head back to the forest and stick together."

The elephants waved their trunks in farewell and stamped around trumpeting to create a diversion as the dragons sped away. The roar of fire engines and shouts from below sounded louder and louder, but fortunately the men were too busy following the smoke and dodging the elephants to notice dragons flying away.

Panting and dripping, they assembled together in mid-air and started back to their forest camp. As they flew, Emily spotted several owls flying in a low straight line towards the trees.

"That's odd," she said breathlessly to Desmond who was close beside her. "Owls don't usually fly like that. They hunt alone."

Desmond grinned. "They aren't used to wide open skies yet, but they'll be OK. They must have found the little hole we melted in the cage just before the trouble started and squeezed through one by one. Good luck to them!"

"What a night!" said Alice sleepily when they reached the camp and found an anxious George waiting for them, "I think it's going to be quite exciting living near you! And there's one good thing: Ollie should be a bit more subdued for a while. I bet his tail's sore."

"Tom will be so excited that he's learned to Huff that he'll soon forget his fright," warned Emily. "I think they'll still cause trouble!"

"The two of us will cope with them between us," said Alice as they settled down.

Chapter 8

The Journey Home

The boys were still quieter than usual the next day, as they started their long journey. They had both received a *very* stern telling off from their Dads, and had been banned from huffing flames until further notice. "You need to learn to treat fire with respect!" Oliver had said. Desmond and the girls had promised not to cause trouble by teasing them about their drenching, so it was quite a peaceful group flying north through low cloud.

All the children had occasional rides, so they made good time. George was a strong flyer despite his age, and baby Georgie was carried in a sling hooked to his mother's spikes, so he slept most of the way. Desmond managed to navigate them back to the camping place by the waterfall as the sun was setting.

They were very tired when they landed, but a refreshing dip in the waterfall pool revived them. Then the children sat on the rocks round the edge, tails and wings dripping, while they watched Des demonstrate the best way to fly through water-falls. It was obvious to Emily and Alice that Ollie was longing to try it himself, but he didn't. Emily thought that Tom looked disappointed in his new-found hero, but none of them said anything about dares (or fires or elephants or haystacks!) as they scrambled back to the campsite to dry out by the fire. Georgie rushed to welcome them. He was bouncing around, full of energy after his sleep, and getting in everyone's way.

Emily noticed Mum and Dad whispering togeth-er as they cooked supper, but she was too hungry to wonder about it for long. Supper was hot rook ris-soles, well-burnt and crunchy, that Ellen had brought from her stores. She also had a bag of dried rose-hips, saved from the previous summer's foraging, which she said were very easy to find in England. Emily thought they were nearly as nice as bumblebugs.

"Why don't we rest here tomorrow, and fly on the day after," Desmond suggested after supper. Emily suspected that he wanted to spend the day flying through the waterfall. Oliver agreed that a rest would be a good idea, especially for George and the children, but Mum and Dad seemed anxious to hurry on.

Ellen seemed to understand. "Why don't we split forces?" she suggested. "Duncan and Gwen can fly on tomorrow and the rest of us can stay here and follow the next day. Des can show us the way, so we won't get lost. They'll get along faster without Tom and Emily."

Tom was delighted, but Emily looked at Mum and Dad and wondered why they wanted to hurry. She made up her mind suddenly. "Can I come with you?" she asked them.

Dad hesitated, but Mum smiled. "Of course you can!" she said. "You fly very well now, and it will be nice to have your help getting the cave ready for visitors. Tom, you can stay, but ONLY if you behave. No showing off under the waterfall and *certainly* no trying to fly through it like Des. Promise?"

"Oh, I don't think we'll have any trouble with these boys at the moment! I think they've learned a lesson," said old George. Ollie tried to pretend he hadn't heard, but Tom blushed. "I promise," he said.

"Couldn't I go with Emily?" asked Alice.

Ellen glanced at Mum. "No, dear, you follow on with the rest of us," she said. "Emily will be waiting for you and you'll have lots of time together when we join them."

"I'll put all my books out for you to see, and collect lots of heather to make your bed," Emily promised the disappointed Alice as they settled down for an early night.

"What's heather?" asked Alice.

Mum, Dad and Emily set off very early next morning while the rest were still asleep. It was sunny and the wind was behind them, helping them along.

"I'd like a word with the otters before the others arrive," Dad said as they flew steadily northwards over the moors. "They were a bit worried that *we* would steal their fish when we arrived at their loch, remember? Then Des came and caused a bit of a fuss, and now *six* more dragons are joining us."

"Lottie and Wattie will love having more of us to play with," said Emily. "And they think Des is great, especially when he gives them rides."

"Their parents might not be very pleased though," said Mum. "I think we should try to find Ellen and Oliver another loch, Duncan. There's a smaller one not far away, with a nice patch of woodland beside it where they could live."

"I want Alice to live with us!" Emily protested.

"No, they want to live near, but not right on top of us. We mustn't try to crowd them out. Let's see how we all get on over the summer. Don't worry, Emily, you'll still see a lot of your new friend."

"Remember, they like travelling, so they might not want to stay permanently," Dad warned.

Emily decided not to think about that. All through the flight she dreamed instead about showing Alice her bedroom, the bats, the otters and the loch. Best of all would be introducing her to Ben, who was her big secret. Surely Mum would let her wake him up to meet SEVEN new dragons!

As they got nearer home, Mum seemed to speed up, even though they were all tired, and when the top of Ben McIlwhinnie's bald head came into sight she seemed full of excitement. As soon as the three of them landed wearily on his boots outside the cave, Mum rushed inside.

Dad smiled at Emily. "We have a secret," he said. "You'll soon know!"

"It's fine!" shouted Mum from inside the cave. "Come and see!"

Dad led Emily into the Bone Cave. Mum was standing beside the big pile of bracken. She pulled some aside to let Emily see. In the middle of the pile was a large Egg!

Emily gasped. "Oh! Is that ours? Are we going to have a hatchling? I never guessed! Is that why we had to hurry home? When will it hatch? Can I feel it? Is it warm?"

Mum laughed at her excited questions. "Yes! I don't think you'll have very long to wait. It's kept beautifully warm while we've been away, and you can hear little scratching noises inside if you get close and listen. Careful though!"

Emily put her ear to the smooth side of the Egg. It was pale blue, with a tracery of golden lines running across the surface, and she thought it was the most beautiful Egg she had ever seen. Sure enough, there were faint movements inside.

"Let's cover it up again," said Mum. "It won't hatch just yet, and we need some food."

Emily thought she would be too excited to eat, but she managed some supper, and then yawned so widely that Mum and Dad said she should go straight to bed.

"I don't suppose I could take the Egg to bed could I?" she asked hopefully. "Just in case it tries to hatch in the night?"

"No," said Mum firmly, "it's coming to bed with us! We'll call you if it starts to crack. You go to sleep. There will be lots to do in the morning."

"You flew really well today," said Dad proudly as he came to tuck her up, and Emily felt very happy as she settled down in her heathery bed. "I do hope it hatches before the others arrive," she thought sleepily. "Just me and Mum and Dad . . ." She closed her eyes.

Chapter 9

The Hatchling

Emily was disappointed to find that the Egg had still not hatched when she got up the next morning. Dad carried it out and placed it carefully beside the fire. The golden tracery sparkled in the sun.

"A watched Egg never hatches!" said Mum. "Let's spend the day getting ready to welcome the others. Duncan, I think you should check out that second loch before we tell the otters."

"As long as you promise to send a huff if there's any sign of a crack," said Dad. They both promised, and he soared away.

"So now you understand why we wanted to hurry back," said Mum to Emily. "We couldn't risk the Egg hatching before we got back. But it was a good idea to leave it in peace to grow, so that was why we went away and left it safely covered up in the cave."

"Did you lay it when we were away with Des and Dad?" Emily asked shyly. "Was that why you didn't come with us?"

"Yes. I wondered if you'd guess, but when you didn't we decided to keep it a secret. You had enough excitement with a friend to look forward to! Now, let's get on with things. The Egg will be fine beside the fire, and we've a lot to do!"

"This is the most exciting week of my life!" Emily declared as she and Mum cleared up and arranged the cave ready for visitors. Dad had been out huffing crows before breakfast and Mum decided to cook them with spicy slug and thistle sauce. Emily collected a lot of nettles and wild thyme, chopped the leaves with beaten pheasant eggs, added some of their precious honey, then poured the mixture into the little Knight moulds that Nan had given to Mum as a present long ago, carefully placing two wild raspberries on each to serve as shield and helmet. She put them to cook in the embers of the fire and checked the Egg while she waited, listening carefully for signs of cracking. She put them into the cave to cool when they were nicely browned and crunchy, and wondered if Alice had ever seen Nettle Knights. There was still a lot to find out about her new friend. She went outside to sneak another peep at the Egg, until Mum sent her off to gather snails.

At lunchtime Dad came back, carrying a load of firewood, and reported that the second loch seemed full of fish, and although he had seen two herons fishing, there were no otters. The woodland came close to the water's edge, and there were several clearings that would make good camp sites. He thought their new friends would be pleased.

They all inspected the Egg hopefully, but there was still no sign of it hatching. Dad turned it round so the other side was near the fire.

It happened just as they were finishing their lunch. There was a sudden loud CRACK! It was followed by a series of sharp taps from inside. A few small holes appeared. Mum, Dad and Emily gathered round. The tapping stopped.

"Can't we help to open it?" whispered Emily. "Perhaps it's stuck."

"No," said Mum, "you must let it crack the shell for itself. It won't be long."

They all stared at the silent Egg, hardly breathing. Then there was a fresh outbreak of tapping and suddenly the shell split in two and a small nose poked out and breathed a little puff of white smoke into the air. Emily gasped. The tiny dragonlet was a bright

golden colour, its long tail was coiled and its wings were folded tightly against its body. Mum leaned down and gave it a very gentle huff, and the baby wriggled free of its shell and huffed back.

"Isn't she beautiful!" breathed Mum, and Dad beamed with pride.

"My little sister!" said Emily. "She is so *tiny*! And I've never seen a *golden* dragonlet before, have you? Can I hold her?"

"Not just yet. Let her stretch her wings. Mum must hold her first. She needs a drink, and then a sleep after all that effort breaking out of her shell."

Emily huffed a kiss, and laughed as the baby wrinkled her nose at her.

"Right Emily, you and I will go down to the loch to warn the otters about our visitors, and leave Mum in peace with the baby for a while. Come on!"

"What shall we call her?" wondered Emily as they flew down the hill. "It will have to be a very special name for a *golden* dragon. Won't Tom be surprised? I can't wait to show Alice!"

"We told Ellen and Oliver. That's why Ellen stopped Alice from coming. She thought we would like to be on our own when the egg hatched. I expect Tom will be pleased not to be the baby of the family anymore."

The otters were waiting for them, and the cubs were delighted to see Emily and very happy to hear that Des, their favourite dragon, was on his way back. They were interested to hear about the new baby, though Lottie and Wattie were surprised to hear that it would be quite a while before she could be taught to swim.

Dad and Emily told them all about their adventures. As he had feared, the otter parents were not very pleased at the prospect of six extra dragons taking fish from their loch but when Dad explained that the new dragons would be fishing in the second loch they calmed down.

When the three grown-ups departed to go fishing, Emily had a chance to tell the cubs about Alice, Ollie and wee Georgie. The story of the park animals and the fire and the elephants took quite a while, and the young otters sat quietly for longer than she'd ever known while they listened.

"Na, ye're inventin' it!" said Wattie when she described the elephants. "They couldn'ae ha' nebs *that* long."

"Did ye no' see any otters in that park thingy?" asked Lottie.

Emily hesitated, then said no. She thought they might be upset if she told them about the pen with the tiny pond. And after all she hadn't actually *seen* the otters who were kept inside, so it wasn't really a lie. Hurriedly she went on to describe the waterfall, and they thought this was almost as good as Desmond's stories of the sea.

As she finished she heard a shout from Dad above her. He pointed to the south, and Emily saw several puffs of white smoke rising above the trees.

"They're nearly here!" he called. "Coming to meet them? We'll tell Mum first, though."

Emily hurriedly said goodbye to the cubs, promising to bring Alice and Ollie to meet them as soon as she could, and flew up to join Dad.

Back at the cave the baby looked quite different. Her wings had dried, her tail had unfurled (it was long with a sparkling golden point) and she was sitting up and looking about her. When Dad and Emily landed, she flapped her wings in excitement and huffed tiny puffs of white smoke.

"Her name is Lily," Mum announced.

Emily put her head down close to the baby. "Hello Lily," she said softly. The baby bounced up and down and squeaked at her and she squeaked back. Mum laughed and said that it would be Emily's job to teach Lily how to speak properly.

"Did you see the signals?" Dad asked Mum. "They're nearly here. Emily and I will go to meet them. Shall we bring them down by the loch? It's quite a crowd to land up here all at once."

"Good idea. I'll bring Lily down when I see them land. Don't tell them – she can be a surprise!"

Chapter 10

Surprises All Round

As soon as Dad and Emily took to the sky they saw the little group of dragons in the distance and flew towards them. Tom was riding on Oliver's back, but as soon as he saw them he climbed off and flew ahead, waving his tail wildly.

"You missed a brilliant time at the waterfall camp!" he shouted to Emily as soon as they were close enough.

"I've had a brilliant time too!" she called back, smiling to herself.

"Follow me down," said Dad to the others. "We'll land by the loch for a drink and a splash and then we'll go up to the cave for a meal. It's nearly ready."

He and Desmond led the others in a slow glide down towards the loch, while Emily found Alice and flew beside her. She was tired, and very pleased to see Emily. "This looks like a lovely place to live," she said, rather breathlessly.

"Wait 'til you see our mountain!" said Emily happily, thinking of all the secrets she had to share. "Nearly there!"

The long line of dragons spiralled down to land on the grassy bank of the loch and dumped their bundles. Ellen let Georgie out of his sling with relief. "He's been wriggling for miles!" she said as Georgie scampered towards the water. "Watch him Ollie! Everything all right?" she asked Dad anxiously.

"Everything's fine!" he assured her. "Any problems on the flight?"

"No, we flew high and kept to the wild places. Scotland's really empty of Humans – it's amazing. We had to dive to avoid a couple of those flying machines of theirs, but they go so fast they wouldn't see what we were."

"What's happened to the otters?" Tom interrupted. "And where's Mum?"

"Here!" said Mum, appearing through the trees. "Look!" She held out baby Lily for everyone to see. Emily laughed to see the astonishment on Tom's face. Ollie and Georgie were splashing in the shallows, watched by George, but everyone else crowded round to admire the baby.

"She's beautiful!" "What a wonderful colour!" "When did she hatch?" "Mum, why didn't you tell me?" "Aaah … huff huff huff …she's so *tiny!*" "This calls for a celebration!" "A party! Let's have a Welcome Party!"

82

The noise made the baby hide under her wings on Mum's hand, but when Old George came quietly over to peer at her, she uncurled and gave him a tiny huff. He beamed with pleasure.

Finally Ollie came across. "What's all the fuss about? Oh a baby, cool, yeah. Coming for a swim, Des?"

All the travellers felt the need of a dip in the loch. Emily took Alice to paddle around by the reeds, and they watched two families of moorhens with their lines of fluffy black chicks dodging in and out. Tom showed off his underwater swimming and diving, and was pleased to find that Ollie couldn't swim nearly as well as he could. All the grown-ups went for a swim, including Mum, who handed Lily over to Dad while she dived in. George gave wee Georgie a swimming lesson in the shallows. There was no sign of the otters, to Tom's surprise, but Emily guessed that they were keeping out of the way until the new-comers calmed down a bit.

Suddenly she saw that Des had flown high, pre-paring for one of his spectacular nose-dives. They all came up to watch as he yelled "DRAGONIMO!!!!"

The otters had been quite close, hidden along the bank, but as Des hit the water there was a burst of cheering from Lottie and Wattie and a disgusted comment from their dad: "Ah kent tha' great daftie'd be back causin' trouble. Him and his fancy spikes!"

They all gathered back on the bank and the otters were introduced to the new dragons. They admired Lily, who had curled up and gone to sleep. Des surfaced and joined them. He looked at Lottie and Wattie in surprise. "You've grown!" he said.

"Course they've grown!" said their mother. "Wee otters grow fast. By next year they'll be big as us an' lookin' for a new loch." Emily and Alice were astonished to hear this. Dragons grow up much more slowly.

"Pity," said Desmond to the cubs. "You'll be too heavy to fly around."

"No bad thing," said their dad.

"Aw, Des!" they yelled together. "We're no' too heavy. Please!"

"OK! On you get. But after this it'll have to be one at a time!" He set off up the loch with the cubs hanging on, and Ellen, Oliver and George watching in astonishment. Des pretended that the cubs were too heavy, and flew slower and lower until they were almost touching the water. Dad shook his head as Ellen looked worried, and sure enough, Des suddenly soared upwards and Ellen gasped as the cubs, shrieking happily, were tipped into the water from quite a height.

Their father sighed heavily. "Nae problem o'er the loch. Ye cannae droon an otter! But ma wee hooligans 're always pesterin' him tae fly them further. O'er the land it'd be anither catch o' fish althigither." Ellen nodded doubtfully, obviously finding it quite hard to understand his broad Scots accent.

Eventually, cooler and cleaner, but very tired, the travellers said goodnight to the otters and set off up the hill to the cave. The huge pot of crow casserole, seasoned with slug and thistle, was simmering over the fire. While it was being dished up, the children looked around inside the cave and Emily proudly showed Alice her room with the precious books on the rock shelf above her bed. They could hear Tom and Ollie hooting in Tom's cave, which had an echo. The bats stayed hidden!

"Let's ask if you can sleep in here tonight," said Emily, as Mum called them out for supper.

The grown-ups discussed the sleeping arrangements after supper, while they enjoyed Emily's nettle knights with their mint tea. She had brought them out in triumph after the crow casserole had been eaten, and Alice had never had anything like them before, so it was a nice surprise. They decided that they would sleep on the ledge outside the cave and find a good camp site in the morning. Emily wondered what they would think if they knew they were camping beside the feet of a sleeping Giant!

Ollie and Alice both decided to sleep inside the cave with Tom and Emily. They were very tired, so after the last nettle knight had been eaten they went to bed without arguing. Alice had never slept on a heather bed before, and found it so comfortable that she fell asleep straight away. Emily lay awake for a little while, listening to her bats and feeling very happy. It had been a wonderful day, and tomorrow would be exciting too!

Chapter 11

The Storm

Everyone got up rather late the next morning, even Georgie. Alice and Emily spent a happy hour looking at Emily's books and talking about their favourites in whispers by the light of Emily's hufftorch, before the boys woke and barged in, wanting them to get up and explore. They went outside to find Ellen stirring porridge, Mum feeding Lily, Oliver sleepily toasting wasp waffles and Dad brewing nettle tea. George had taken Georgie for a short walk by the stream to keep him out of the way. There was no sign of Desmond.

Over breakfast, Emily remembered the idea of a Welcome Party, and everyone agreed it was an excellent plan.

"You'll all have to help. We can build a big fire and have a barbecue," said Mum.

"Can the Otters come?" asked Tom.

"I don't think they'd manage to climb right up here," said Dad.

"I know!" said Emily, who had the beginnings of an idea. "We could have the barbecue a bit further down the hill." She pointed. "Just there, on the flat bit. The otters should be able to get as far as that." The spot she meant was *exactly* where they had all landed in a heap when Ben McIlwhinnie first woke up and sneezed, the day they had found their new cave.

Mum looked at her, and guessed what was in her mind. "Good idea!" she said. "We'll have it tomorrow evening. Today we have to go down to explore the new loch and find a good place for you to camp for the summer."

"And we'll need lots of foraging and fishing for such a big barbecue," added Ellen.

"And hunting," said Oliver. "There seem to be plenty of rabbits round here. It's a great place you've found!"

"Wherever has Des got to?" Emily wondered. "He hasn't gone off travelling already, has he?"

"He's left all his things," said Mum, "so I'm sure he'll be back."

Emily managed a private word with Mum before they set off down to the second loch. "We can wake Ben, can't we?" she pleaded. "He did say we could if nice things happened. There's such a lot of exciting things to tell him, and so many new dragons for him to meet. And he would *definitely* want to see Lily, I know he would. PLEASE!"

"I suppose you want to wake him and give everyone a surprise at the barbecue. Is that why you wanted it down there? It's certainly the best view of Ben! All right – I'm sure he won't mind as it's such an important party."

"Thanks Mum! I'm going to tell Des, when he turns up, and make sure he keeps the secret."

They were halfway to the second loch when Emily spotted Des flying down the mountain-side towards them, and flew to meet him. She managed a breathless whisper before they joined the others. Desmond, who explained that he had been up the mountain 'for a recce', was delighted at the thought of meeting the ancient Mountain Giant at last, and promised not to breathe a word to the others.

They all went down together to explore the woods by the new loch, and found a perfect place for a camp, in a lovely glade with a clump of spreading oak trees for shelter when it rained. Alice had enjoyed spending the night with Emily, but said she really preferred sleeping out of doors, and Emily had to agree that her room was a bit small for two.

"When we're settled you can come and have a sleepover with me," Alice said. "I think Mum, Dad and Grandad will be happy to stay here for the whole summer. I hope so. I think it's great, and Ollie does too. He can't wait to learn to swim and dive as well as Des."

"You mean better than Tom!" said Emily, and they both giggled as Ollie turned and scowled at them. But he was too happy with their new home to pick a fight, and they went off to explore the woods together, leaving the grown-ups in peace to set up their new home.

It was an unusually hot day for the Highlands, but as the afternoon wore on, huge purple clouds began to pile up in the west. Desmond came to find the children. "We're all heading back to the cave," he said. "It looks as though we're in for a thunderstorm."

He was right. They had just reached the cave when they heard the first rumble of thunder, and a few minutes later heavy drops of rain fell. They all crouched in the cave gazing out at the brilliant flashes of lightning that lit up the hills, and shouting to make themselves heard over the thunder crashes. The rain poured down until the stream became a torrent and thundered down to the loch. Little Georgie was frightened and hid behind his dad, but the four youngsters danced around in the rain, too wet to huff but singing loudly. Amazingly, Lily slept through all the noise.

When the storm passed it was nearly dark. Emily's bats woke and flew out to hunt, complaining about the crowded cave in their high squeaky voices. The rain was still falling, though much less heavily, so they had all agreed that the cave was the best place to spend the night. It was all right for the children, who went cheerfully back to their rooms for another night, but the grown-ups found the main cave a bit of a squash, even though it was warm and dry!

In the middle of the night, Desmond woke. It was far too hot inside the cave, so he flew up to sit on Ben's head and stare at the stars. The rain had stopped, the moon had risen and the night smelled of damp bracken. He felt restless. It had been fun meeting all these new dragons and exploring this lovely bit of the Highlands, but there was so much of the world left to see. There were more mountains – higher ones – to the north. He would stay for the party, meet Ben and then he would set off on his travels again, he decided. Emily wouldn't miss him now she had Alice. He took off happily for a moonlight flight instead of settling back to sleep.

Chapter 12

The Welcome Party

The next day there was no time for any more exploring. All the dragons had their jobs to do. There was hunting and fishing, and collecting as much dry wood as they could find among the trees. Emily and Alice went foraging, found a patch of wild strawberries and some early raspberries, and collected a big bagful. The boys collected mushrooms, found some weirdly shaped golden fungi in the woods, and then hunted for hornets to toast on sticks over the fire. Ollie said they were delicious dipped in honey, which Ellen supplied from her stores. Dad and Oliver concocted a special brew of Firewater for the grown-ups, and Mum made Ginger Fizz for the youngsters. Des mixed one of his extra-spicy sauces to go with sizzling snake sausages and rabbit chunks on sticks. ("Those red pods should be called Hotties, not Chillies!" said Ollie after tasting one, trying to cool a burning tongue.)

They built a big fire on the flat place that Emily had chosen and invited the otters, who agreed they could easily lollop that far. Nobody had time to look up at the mountain and notice what an odd shape it was!

As the sun dropped lower in the sky, they lit the fire and the smell of the barbecue began to drift up towards the mountain and down towards the loch. The otters arrived, rather out of breath, sniffed the fish burning on the barbeque and asked if they could have theirs raw. The dragons tucked in to the spicy barbecued food, getting more and more sticky and huffing hotter and hotter flames. Tingling tongues were hung out to cool. The young otters tried Hot Hornets *and* Chilli Dip, and had to be dunked in the stream to cool off. "Ye're *otters*, ye wee eejits! Ye cannae eat tha' fiery stuff!" said their Dad as he held their heads under. Alice and Emily discovered that the boys had eaten more than their fair share of wild strawberries, but were too happy – and much too full – to be very annoyed.

Finally, replete and happy, they sat in a ring round the fire. Dad proposed a toast to their new neighbours. Ellen proposed a toast to baby Lily. Tom shouted that they should toast Des, because he had found their new friends, but Des (who was blushing and looking even more colourful than usual) said it had all been Emily's idea and *she* deserved a toast the most! She blushed too, so they all raised their mugs of Firewater and Ginger Fizz, cheered loudly and toasted everyone, even the otters.

Then Emily sprang her big surprise. "Everyone look at the mountain!" she cried and, as they all turned, Mum, Dad and Desmond gathered together and gently huffed the smoke from the barbecue towards Ben McIlwhinnie. The nose twitched, the ears waggled and slowly the huge eyes blinked open.

"It's a real live Giant!" breathed Ollie. "Wow!"

"Is it safe?" whispered Ellen.

"Never in my long life have I met a Giant!" said old George in wonder.

Ben beamed at the little group below him. "Well I never! A Conflagration of Dragons! And what a rainbow

– orange and turquoise, red and green and every shade of Scottish blue! Otters too! Are you ALL coming to live on my mountain? No, don't all try to tell me at the same time! I think I would like EMILY to explain."

Bursting with pride, Emily told him about the Gloaming Huff, the arrival of Desmond and the journey south to meet the new family and bring them to live in the Highlands. "They're going to live near the other loch so they don't disturb the otters too much," she said, and Ben nodded his approval. "And the biggest news of all," she finished, "is that we have a new baby, only three days old! I was there when she hatched. Look!" Mum held Lily up high for Ben to see.

Ben peered down at the tiny dragonlet. "A golden dragon!" he exclaimed. "She will grow up to be rare and beautiful. Bring her to me for a closer look." Mum and Dad flew up to Ben's hand with Lily and were carried to the level of his face. Lily sat up and gave a tiny huff and Ben beamed at her in delight before carefully lowering his hand.

"This is SO cool!" breathed Ollie, "D'you think he'd give us all a ride up there?"

"Aye, us too!" shouted the little otters, but were firmly told to stay on the ground by their mother, in case they wobbled and fell off.

To Ollie's delight, Ben said, "Now Emily and Tom and their new friends," and the four of them rushed to climb aboard Ben's hand and be introduced properly. Alice and Ollie were both rather shy when they came so close to Ben, and when Tom showed off his favourite perch on Ben's ear they were most

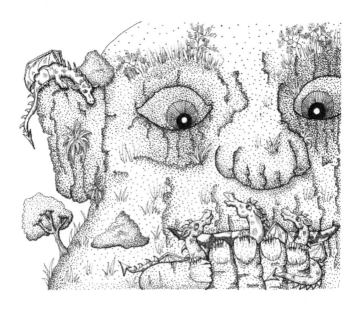

impressed. Emily got a special smile and a wink of one huge eye before they were lowered down. Then Ellen and Oliver took Georgie, keeping a firm hold as he was bouncing with excitement, and finally Desmond and George travelled up to speak to the giant.

"So you are the messenger," Ben said to Desmond, who beamed with pride. "It is because you are a Traveller that you brought these dragon families together to be neighbours and friends. Well done! And you, George, must also have travelled far and seen much in your long life, and I would value a talk with you." George promised to fly up for a long conversation the very next day, while Ben was still awake.

"Now that I have met you all, back to your banquet! It smells delicious," Ben declared, and he was delighted when Emily flew up to give him the last three Honeyed Hornets, and Des to pour a large measure of Dad's special Firewater into his mouth.

As the moon rose, they danced the Dragon Reel round the dying fire, and then Lily was carried off to bed, already fast asleep. The otters said goodnight as well, waved to Ben and lolloped back to the loch, the cubs still steaming gently. Ellen and Oliver gathered their family together for the short flight back to their camp, despite Ollie's protests that he wasn't the least bit tired.

"See you tomorrow!" called Alice to Emily, waving as they set off. Emily waved back feeling very happy.

Dad took Tom, protesting sleepily, to bed, and Des and Emily were left by the fire.

"Well done, Emily!" Ben's deep voice echoed softly through the darkness. "All this has happened because *you* wanted a friend so much! You believed in the Gloaming Huff, so you kept trying even when others had given up, and that brought young Desmond the Traveller. You found Alice and her family and brought them here, and now you have a sister as well. I am so glad you woke me up to share all this good news."

"I love having friends. We're all going to spend the summer together. It's going to be such fun!" said Emily happily.

"Not me. I'll be going travelling again very soon," Des said quietly.

"Oh no!" she said. "Don't go! You're my friend too."

"I won't be going straight away! And I'll still be your friend, however far I travel," Des promised. "I'll come back to see you and Tom and the others, don't worry. You have Alice now, and Ollie. I don't think you're going to be lonely this summer!"

"And you have me," said Ben. "I will be your friend as long as you live, even when I'm asleep. You can wake me up whenever you need me!"

"Emily!" called Mum from the cave entrance. "It's long past your bedtime!"

"Goodnight Emily, sleep well," said Desmond, giving her a Huff and a hug, and he flew up to Ben's bald head to watch the moon rise and dream of his travels.

Emily blew them both a big Huff and went happily into the cave to join her family. She peeped at sleeping Lily and heard Tom rustling his bed as he settled down. "It's been a magic day and it was a lovely party," she said, hugging her Mum and Dad in turn. She yawned, snuggling into her heather. "Tomorrow I'll go and see Alice and we'll…"

She fell asleep.

END OF BOOK TWO

Des, the wild Travelling Dragon, takes far too many risks.

His travels are full of narrow escapes: Humans, whales, seals, volcanos....

While he is away, Emily and Tom have an exciting summer with Alice and Ollie. And when he returns, things get even more adventurous!

Share Emily and Tom's summer in *Dragon Tales Book III: Quest for Adventure* by Judy Hayman.

Coming soon.

What Dragons

Food they forage

birds eggs (only one from each nest.)

beetles

wild strawberrys and raspberrys

Slugs

mushrooms

fungi

rose hips

Snails

toad stools?

(poisonous but not to dragons.)

elder berries

Hot meals

spicy slug stew

rook rissoles (Ellen's recipe.)

crow casserole (seasoned with slug and thistle)

beetle broth

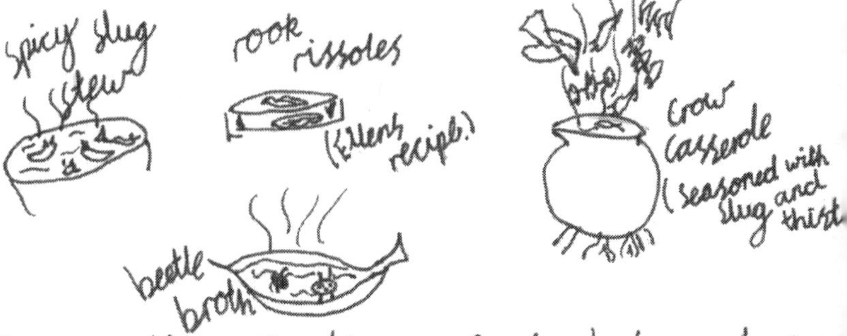

Dragons like all their food hot and spicy

Like to Eat . . . by Elise Hayman aged 11

Snacks and drinks

nettle knights (made by Emily in her granny moulds)

bumble bugs (Des's favourite)

(Ellens) wasp waffles

bramble biscuits (burnt)

hot honeyed hornets

nettle or mint tea

fire water (adults only!)

ginger fizz

On the barbecue

Des's dip

fish (bones and all.)

rabbit chunks

snake sausages

very VERY spicy!

ey also like things burnt and crunchy.

Acknowledgements

To all my family: Kate and Roddy, Rachel and Brendan, Martin and Eleanor, who have given such support and encouragement; Peter for much-needed technical assistance; grandchildren Phoebe, Elise, David, Sam and Megan for lots of good ideas, and for helping to launch Book 1.

To all the friends who have helped to spread the word about Book 1, and told me what bits their children and grandchildren liked best.

As always, to Alison, who has produced another lovely book with such efficiency and style.

And of course to Caroline, whose dragons keep getting more and more lively and lovely!

About the author

Judy Hayman lives with her husband Peter on the edge of the Lammermuir Hills in East Lothian, Scotland, where there is a wonderful view and plenty of wildlife, but no dragons, as far as she knows. At various times in her past life she has taught English in a big comprehensive school; written plays, directed and occasionally acted for amateur theatre companies; been a Parliamentary candidate for both Westminster and the Scottish Parliament; and a Mum. Sometimes all at once. Now preventing the Lammermuirs from taking over her garden and being a Gran takes up a lot of time, and fits well with writing these Dragon Tales.

About the illustrator

 Caroline Wolfe Murray studied Archaeology at the University of Edinburgh and took a career path in the field, turning her hand to archaeological illustration. She has always had a passion for exploration and discovery which evolved from her experience of living in Spain, Belgium, Venezuela and New Zealand. She now resides in East Lothian with her husband James and her two young daughters Lily and Mabel, who have been her inspiration to work on a children's book.

Read on for the first chapter of Dragon Tales Book III: Quest for Adventure, *coming soon…*

Chapter 1

All About Islands

In the middle of summer in the Highlands of Scotland it scarcely goes dark all night. On fine evenings the sky is a clear blue, a few stars can be seen, the moon rises huge on the horizon and there is a line of light low in the North and West. Emily and Tom, who had always lived there, were used to this but their friends Alice and Ollie had only just arrived in the Highlands from England, and still found it surprising.

The very best thing about summer, as the four young dragons had discovered, was that their parents *sometimes* forgot about bedtime. When it was raining they remembered, and shooed the children off to bed; but on fine evenings like this one, if the four older ones slipped away somewhere they could get away with several extra hours after the little ones, Georgie and Lily, were safely in bed.

This evening they had crept away from Ollie and Alice's home in the wood by the small loch, leaving their four parents talking by the fire. Sometimes Des, their Traveller friend, stayed but often he forgot he was grown up and snuck away with the children. And tonight was special; they had arranged to wake Ben.

They had forgotten everything but the enthralling tales Ben was telling them. As the sky darkened slowly and more stars appeared, Ben's deep voice went on and on. Desmond was sitting quite still on the top of Ben's bald head, listening and gazing into the distance. Tom and Ollie were perched as usual on Ben's ears, though Ollie, who was quite a bit bigger than Tom, was finding it hard to keep his balance. Emily and Alice were sitting comfortably together on Ben's huge hand, which he had raised up in front of his face.

110

Ben was an ancient Mountain Giant who had spent centuries asleep on this spot until he had almost become part of the landscape. In the last few months, with the arrival of Emily's family, who had moved into the cave beneath his chair, and then the English dragons a few weeks later, he had spent more time awake than he had done for centuries. It was young company, he explained. There was so much going on! The children had discovered that he didn't really mind if they huffed gently up his nose to wake him up on fine evenings. They had learnt not to huff too hard. One giant sneeze could send little dragons whirling through the air in quite a dangerous way!

"Did you know all this land was once covered with ice and snow all year round?" Ben was saying. "Even the sea was frozen. Giants could walk for days and see nothing else alive. I tried it for a hundred years or so, but then it seemed like a good time to sleep! So that's what I did. And when I next awoke the ice was gone and the land was green. My legs were younger then, so I walked North over the mountains until I reached the sea. And far over the sea there

111

were islands, hummocky and green. I wanted to reach them, so I started to walk through the sea. Deeper and deeper I went, to my knees, to my waist, and finally to my shoulders. I looked back and I was a long way from the land, but the islands were still far off. What should I do? Even a mountain giant can drown. By this time white waves were tickling my chin!"

"Islands," said Des dreamily from Ben's head. "I love flying to islands..."

"It's easy if you have wings! Unfortunately that's one thing giants don't have," said Ben.

"There wouldn't be any Horrible Humans on an island," said Ollie. "They can't fly either. Go on, Ben."

"That's where you're wrong, young Oliver, as I soon found out," Ben continued. "I turned my head this way and that...." He demonstrated, making the boys on his ears wobble and Ollie flap his wings to keep his balance. "...and I saw, coming towards me, six humans bouncing over the waves in a ..."

"Boat!" shouted Emily and Alice together. They had read about boats in their books.

"Quite right! They were moving so fast that if I had opened my mouth wide they might have shot in!"

"Yuk!" said Tom, but the others shushed him, wanting Ben to continue.

"Suddenly they realised I was there. I heard screams. The boat lurched and I feared they would fall overboard and drown. But they righted themselves and rowed towards the nearest island as fast as they could. I stood and watched them. The boat looked like a tiny insect with many long legs as it disappeared into the distance. Then I saw wee people gathered on the shore waving and shouting and I realised they could see my head in the sea. I have often wondered what legends they made up about the strange moving rock that appeared one day in the middle of the sea and vanished the next!"

The children chuckled, but Des had a serious question.

"Ben, I've heard of an island that's a home of many dragons far off to the North West. Do you know about that?"

"I did walk further round the shore and saw more islands to the west, but always the sea was too deep for me to reach them. But once I saw, far far away over the sea, a huge plume of grey smoke and tongues of fire rising high in the sky."

"That's it!" said Desmond excitedly. "There are huge dragons living in caves there, and from time to time they wake up and breathe out fire and smoke. I spoke once with an old Traveller who'd been there. The big dragons were asleep, but he said over all the land you could see little huffs of dragon breath floating through the air. It must be a magical place."

Listening to his voice, Emily realised that the urge to travel was getting stronger and stronger in her friend Desmond. He had stayed with them longer than he had intended, but he was obviously getting itchy wings as he listened to Ben. She hated the thought of waving goodbye to him. He was such good company, with his coloured spikes and his fancy cooking, his love of exploring and the wild tales of his adventures.

"Hmm," came Ben's voice, "I have never been there, of course, but I believe the place is called Ice Land and is far out in the Western sea. Chilly by the sound of it, and so NOT a suitable place for dragons." He rolled his eyes to look up at Des and gave a deep rumbling chuckle. "Tell me all about it when you get back," he said, and closed his eyes.

"Des, you can't go!" said all the young dragons together.

"I must, I'm a Traveller – and I've stayed here far too long! I really like the sound of this Ice Land place." He yawned widely. "Needs a bit of planning. Tomorrow. Come on, you'd better go down before they start looking for you."

They said goodnight to Ben - who waved his hand with his eyes shut once Emily and Alice had flown up - and made their way home; Alice and Ollie to their woodland camp and Emily and Tom to their cave.

"See you tomorrow," said Alice as they left. Des waved to them, then disappeared inside the grubby bag he slept in and said no more about plans or islands.

It had been a lovely evening, Emily thought as she snuggled down in her heather bed. But the thought of losing Desmond had spoiled it. It was a long time before she fell asleep, and when she did she dreamed of islands that smoked and the wide wild sea.

For more information on the Dragon Tales books, email info@alisonjones.com

116